GROSSET & DUNLAP
An Imprint of Penguin Random House LLC, New York

Adapted by Laura Stiers

ROALD DAHL

www.roalddahl.com

Visit us online at www.penguinrandomhouse.com.

ISBN 9780593097113   10 9 8 7 6 5 4 3 2 1

ROALD DAHL

THE WITCHES

How to SPOT A WITCH

ILLUSTRATED BY Carmi Grau

Grosset & Dunlap

THIS IS NOT A
FAIRY-TALE.
THIS IS ABOUT
REAL WITCHES.

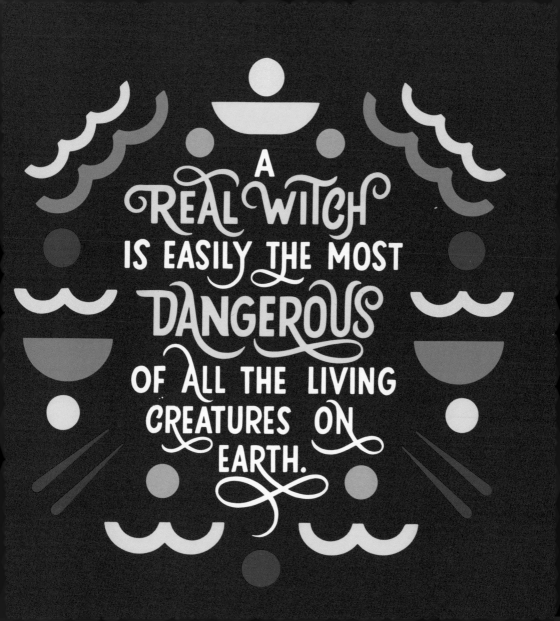

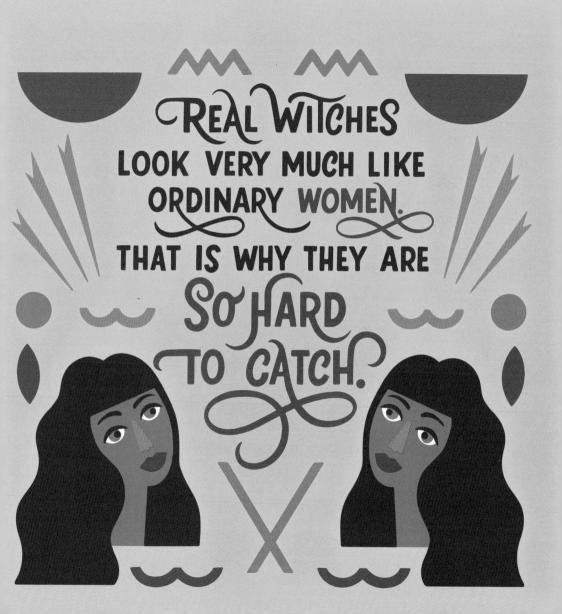

A REAL WITCH HATES CHILDREN WITH A RED-HOT SIZZLING HATRED.

SHE HAS MAGIC IN HER FINGERS AND DEVILRY DANCING IN HER BLOOD.

A
REAL WITCH
IS ALWAYS
BALD.

BALD AS A
BOILED EGG.

THEIR
SPIT IS BLUE.
BLUE AS A
BILBERRY.

A REAL WITCH
HAS THE MOST
AMAZING POWERS
OF SMELL.

LOOK FOR THE NOSE-HOLES... LIKE THE RIM OF A CERTAIN KIND OF SEASHELL.

SHE CAN ACTUALLY SMELL OUT A CHILD WHO IS STANDING ON THE OTHER SIDE OF THE STREET ON A PITCH-BLACK NIGHT.

HER MIND WILL
ALWAYS BE
PLOTTING
AND SCHEMING
AND
CHURNING
AND BURNING

AND WHIZZING AND PHIZZING WITH MURDEROUS BLOODTHIRSTY THOUGHTS.

WHEREVER YOU FIND
PEOPLE,
YOU FIND WITCHES.
AND
WHATEVER HAPPENS,

YOU MUSTN'T
LET THEM
CATCH YOU.

THAT'S ABOUT ALL I CAN TELL YOU. NONE OF IT IS VERY HELPFUL.

EVEN WHEN
YOU KNOW ALL THE
SECRETS,
YOU CAN STILL NEVER
BE QUITE SURE WHETHER IT IS
A WITCH
YOU ARE GAZING AT
OR JUST A
KIND LADY.

IF SHE HAS
ALL OF THESE THINGS,
THEN YOU
RUN LIKE
MAD.